SAY NO AND FLY AWAY!

A
FABLES FROM THE LETTER PEOPLE
BOOK

WRITTEN BY:
ELAYNE REISS-WEIMANN
RITA FRIEDMAN

ILLUSTRATED BY:
ELIZABETH CALLEN

NEW DIMENSIONS IN EDUCATION, INC.
50 EXECUTIVE BLVD.
ELMSFORD, NY 10523

Printed in U.S.A.

ISBN 0-89796-013-0

1 2 3 4 5 6 7 8 9 0   SPC   SPC   89098   13514

Nellie Nuthatch and her four nuthatches
are Mr. N's friends.
Mr. N helped Nellie take care of the nuthatches
when they were babies.
Mr. N loves the nuthatches.
The nuthatches love Mr. N.

One day Nellie Nuthatch has to fly north
for a short visit.
"My nuthatches are old enough to take care
of themselves now," Nellie says to Mr. N.
"But I do not want them to fly about late at night.
Can you please check to see if they are
in the birdhouse at bedtime?"
"I'm happy to help," says Mr. N.
"I can sit under the tree near the birdhouse tonight."
"You may if you want to," says Nellie,
"but it is not necessary.
The nuthatches are not babies anymore."

Nellie flies away.

Mr. N says to the nuthatches, "I'll be back
at bedtime.

Tonight I will sit under your tree."

"It will be fun to have Mr. N sit under our tree,
the way he did when we were babies,"
says one nuthatch.

"No it won't," says Newly Nuthatch.

"We won't be able to fly around and stay up late.
But I know a way to keep Mr. N busy.
Follow me," says Newly.

The nuthatches follow Newly to Mr. N's house.

"Take the numerals off Mr. N's house," says Newly.

"Wait! These numerals do not belong to us,"

say the nuthatches.

"It does not matter," says Newly.

"We are only borrowing them.

Never mind. You are babies!

I'll do it myself."

Newly takes the numerals off Mr. N's house.

Newly flies from house to house, removing numerals.

"Newly, are you sure it is not wrong

to take the numerals?" ask the nuthatches.

"There is nothing wrong with borrowing," says Newly.

"Well, then we will help you," say the nuthatches.

All afternoon the nuthatches fill bags with numerals.

"Put all the numerals in the tree," says Newly.

"Then go into the birdhouse.

When you hear Mr. N, pretend you are asleep."

Before long, the nuthatches hear Mr. N's noisy nose.

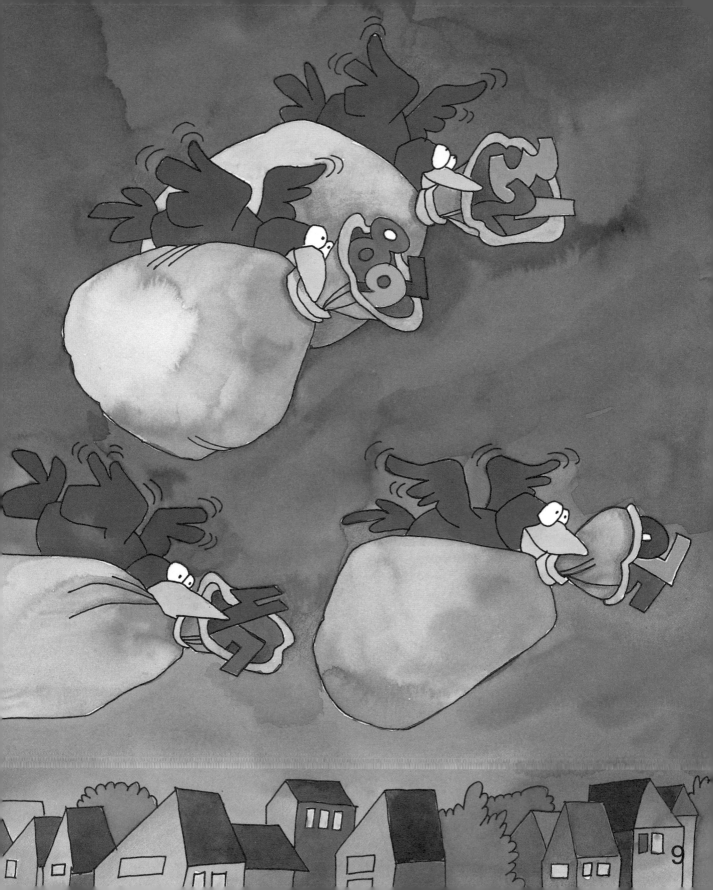

Mr. N looks inside the birdhouse.

"The nuthatches are asleep," he says.

Newly waits until Mr. N sits down under the tree.

Then he starts to drop the numerals.

Numerals fall all around Mr. N.

Mr. N runs this way and that, trying to catch
the numerals.

"These numerals come from people's houses,"
says Mr. N.

"I need to find out where they belong."

"See," whispers Newly, "now Mr. N will be busy
all night.

We can fly about and stay up late."

Mr. N walks from one neighbor's house
to the next neighbor's house.
Everywhere he looks, numerals are missing
from the houses.
"I'll try to put all the numerals back where they
belong," says Mr. N.
He works and works.
It is dark and he is tired.
Mr. N makes many mistakes.
The next morning people have wrong addresses.
Mr. N sleeps until noon.
He does not know the confusion the wrong addresses
cause.

13

The Ning's newspaper is delivered
to the Nettle's house.
The Newberry's mail is put in the Navarro's mailbox.
Mr. N's neighbors telephone him.
"Mr. N," they say, "why do you have the right address
on your house but we do not?"
"I must have put the wrong numerals on your
houses," says Mr. N.
"Mr. N, why did you take the numerals off our
houses?" ask his neighbors.
Mr. N explains how the numerals fell around him.
"How strange," say the neighbors.
"Let's work together to put the numerals back where
they belong."
The neighbors work together.
Soon everyone has the right address again.

15

The nuthatches sleep all day.

They do not know about the wrong addresses.

When they awaken, they say, "Newly, we want to be sure all the numerals are back on the houses."

The nuthatches fly from house to house.

"See," says Newly Nuthatch, "I told you nothing bad would happen.

The numerals are back where they belong."

"Newly, we are still not sure it is right to borrow numerals," say the nuthatches.

"Don't be babies!

Do what I say," insists Newly.

Just then a clock strikes.

"Let's take numerals off all the outdoor clocks,"
says Newly.

"Then we'll have numerals to drop on Mr. N tonight."

"Newly, I don't think we should listen to you,"
says one of the nuthatches.

"You are a baby!" says Newly.

Not one of the nuthatches wants to be called a baby.
They are afraid to say no to Newly.
The nuthatches remove all the numerals
from all the clocks.
They take the numerals back to the tree.
Later that night, Mr. N sits under the tree.
Soon numerals start falling all around him.
"Why do numerals fall around me night after night?"
wonders Mr. N.
"People will think I am removing the numerals."

21

The nuthatches see Mr. N is upset.

"Newly, we must tell Mr. N we borrowed the numerals," they say.

"No," says Newly, "I do not want to get into trouble.

Let everyone think Mr. N took the numerals."

"Newly, this time we won't listen to you.

We know you are wrong," say the nuthatches.

"You are all babies," says Newly.

"We don't care what you call us," answer the nuthatches.

They fly down to Mr. N.

Newly Nuthatch flies away as fast as he can.

The nuthatches tell Mr. N what they did.

"I am glad you are telling me the truth," says Mr. N.

"It is wrong to take anything that does not belong to you.

It is wrong to borrow unless you ask permission first."

"Newly made us do it," say the nuthatches.

"He called us babies.

It is all Newly's fault."

"Newly was wrong and I will speak to him," says Mr. N, "but each of you was wrong too."

25

"Listen to me very carefully," says Mr. N.

"Never, ever do anything you think may be wrong.

"Don't care if someone calls you a baby.

You are a big bird, not a baby, when you refuse to do something wrong.

Don't be afraid to say NO.

Say NO and fly away."

"Watch us, Mr. N," say the nuthatches.

"This is what we'll do next time."

Mr. N watches.

The nuthatches say NO and fly away.

27

The next day the nuthatches fly to Mr. N's house.

"Mr. N, may we borrow something from you
if we ask permission first?" ask the nuthatches.

"Yes, of course," says Mr. N.

"What would you like to borrow?"

"You have a box filled with letters of the alphabet.
May we borrow some of the letters?"

"Are you going to put letters on the clocks instead
of numerals?" asks Mr. N.

"No," say the nuthatches.

"Newly wants to put the numerals back
on the clocks all by himself.
Newly is sorry he was naughty.
We need the letters for a very important reason.
Look up into the sky tomorrow and you'll see."

The next morning an unusual cloud floats in the sky.
On it is this message from the nuthatches: